Other Titles Available:

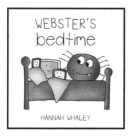
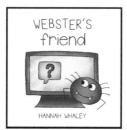
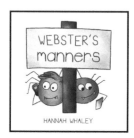

For Layla and Iris

Published by Born Digital Books.

www.borndigitalbooks.co.uk

Text © 2013 by Hannah Whaley.
Illustrations © 2013 by Hannah Whaley.

First printing: August 2014.
Rudiment Font © Kevin Richey

ISBN-13: 978-0-9930012-0-8

Webster's Email

Written and Illustrated
by Hannah Whaley

Webster's baby sister Ivy
always looked delightful

...until a camera flashed one day,
and caught her looking frightful!

She looked a silly baby,
and Webster chuckled
with delight.

The picture that he'd taken
was such a funny sight!

He decided he would email it.
He clicked and it was gone.

Daddy saw it straight away,
and that was number one.

Daddy sent it on to Grandma,
he thought she'd like to see.

Grandma passed it on to Grandad
so they were two and three.

Number four was Uncle Percy who saw it on his phone. He emailed it to Cousin Sue...

But Sue was not alone!

Now Cousin Sue was number five.
Her friend was number six.

They thought they'd pass it on once more -
it went in two more clicks.

Bertie Bat and Bobbie Bat
were numbers seven and eight.

Webster wished he could stop it now
but it was far too late!

For they sent it on to Mummy Bat,
and she was number nine.

She laughed and laughed out loud and said
"I'm glad she isn't mine!"

She sent it on to number ten -
her good friend Betty Bee.

She shared it round her tea party
for everyone to see.

The girls she sent it to all giggled:
eleven, twelve, thirteen. Who can they send it to
they wondered? Who hasn't already seen?

So it arrived with Roger Frog who put it on his big screen. Ivy looked even funnier now, and he became fourteen.

Roger Frog had three sweet daughters –
April, Maisy and Charlene.

So he forwarded it on three times:
fifteen, sixteen, seventeen.

They sniggered at Ivy's funny face...

Webster didn't know
what to do.

Although he chose to email it,
he wished he'd thought it through.

For soon their piano teacher, Miss Bug,
saw her phone flash beside her.

But she was friends with Webster's Mummy and
she knew that little spider!

So she sent it on straight away
(Miss Bug was now eighteen)

But it went right to Webster's Mummy,
who didn't know she was nineteen!

Webster hoped Mum wasn't cross with him.
He hoped she wasn't mad.

He hadn't meant to cause this fuss
when he emailed it to Dad.

Then suddenly, his computer beeped!
It was a message from his Mummy!

He opened the email up and read:
"I think you'll find this funny..."

There was Ivy's silly face –
the one that Webster took.
Mummy wasn't cross at all,
she thought he'd like a look.

His email had come
back to him.
Webster was number twenty.

But he didn't send it on again -
they decided twenty's plenty.

CPSIA information can be obtained
at www.ICGtesting.com
Printed in the USA
LVHW070236210919
631814LV00010B/78/P

9 780099 300120 8